MARGARET MORGAN
and
MARY MORGAN PEDLOW

Memorial

RIVERSIDE PUBLIC LIBRARY

BAMBOO

For my mother, Gum-may, who knew China and farmed its land. - P.Y.

Published in 2006 in the US by
SIMPLY READ BOOKS

www.simplyreadbooks.com

Text copyright © 2006 by Paul Yee
Illustrations copyright © 2006 by Shaoli Wang
Book design by Jacqueline Wang

The text of this book is set in ITC Galliard

10 9 8 7 6 5 4 3 2 1

Printed in Korea

ISBN 1-894965-53-1

CIP data available from The Library of Congress

BAMBOO

By Paul Yee   Illustrated by Shaoli Wang

SIMPLY READ BOOKS

One day, Bamboo, a young farmer, took
two baskets of beans to sell at the market.
There, peasants from far and wide traded
fresh fruit and greens, farm animals and
the latest news.

Amidst the noise and heat, Bamboo was enchanted by one girl's beautiful smile. He thought about her all the way home.

Bamboo told his older brother, Banyan, about the cheerful farm girl, Ming.

"She will make a good wife and bring our family luck," Bamboo said.

Banyan encouraged Bamboo, but Banyan's wife, Jin, disliked Ming from the day they met. Nevertheless, the two families agreed on marriage plans for Bamboo and Ming.

At the wedding, Ming presented Bamboo with a special gift.

"Bamboo seedlings!" her new husband exclaimed.

"Yes, we'll plant them and watch them spring to life and fill the sky."

By morning, new shoots were nudging up, and by the next day the stalks were tall and thick. In no time at all, a bamboo grove flourished.

At breakfast Jin complained, "I hate getting up at dawn."

"When the rooster crows," Ming answered, "the air blows fresh and cool. It's the best time of all."

"She's right," agreed Banyan and Bamboo.

After working in the field all day, Jin grumbled, "Farm life is such a burden. My back hurts, and my hands and feet are cracked. No wonder the townspeople laugh at us."

"Yes," Ming agreed, "the work is hard and the townspeople scorn us. But they feast on the food we grow and can't live without us."

Again the two brothers agreed with her.

When Jin gave birth to a son, Bamboo decided to go to the New World to earn money to buy more land for their growing family.

"You are wise and will do well," Ming said to him. "Come home safely."

"I'll return soon," Bamboo promised. "You're my greatest joy."

As soon as Bamboo left, Jin said to Banyan, "We must divide the fields."

"But this is family land, and it belongs to all of us."

"Bamboo will return a rich man," Jin mocked. "Worry about your wife and son."

So Banyan and Jin took the best fields, along with the plough and the buffalo.

   Ming was only given the bamboo patch, an old water-wheel and a hut to live in. She had no tools to work the land.

But Ming wasn't worried. She cut some bamboo poles to till the soil. To her amazement, they jumped to life and began to plough the earth into neat furrows ready for planting, with no help from any human hand.

At the end of the day Jin smirked, "So, how much land did you till today?"

"I'm almost finished," Ming said.

Filled with curiosity, Jin decided to find out how Ming got so much work done in a day.

The next morning Jin secretly watched Ming at work in her field. When she saw the bamboo tilling the soil, Jin thought, *Those bamboo poles are magic! I must have them for myself.*

That evening Jin crept into Ming's field and tried to steal the magic bamboo. But the poles leapt up and beat her.

"Yow! Yow! Yow!" she yelped.

Jin ran home to her husband and wailed, "Sister-in-law used her bamboo poles to beat me! You must destroy them!"

"Leave Ming alone!" Banyan protested.

"Do as I say," Jin hissed, "or I'll tell the whole village you're a coward who refuses to protect his wife."

Under the moonlight, Banyan gathered up the bamboo poles, threw them into the river and watched the swift waters carry them away.

The next morning Ming couldn't find her bamboo poles anywhere. She cut down a new pole to carry the water buckets to the creek.

It will take days to irrigate this field, she thought, as she pedalled the creaky old water-wheel.

To her surprise, water began to flow up through the bamboo pole onto the higher land. Soon all her work was done.

From her hiding place, Jin saw everything and was furious.

When Jin got home, she smeared charcoal on her face and hands to look like bruises.

"Sister-in-law beat me with another bamboo pole!" she wailed to Banyan. "Look at all these bruises! This time make sure you destroy the entire grove of bamboo!"

"I told you to leave Ming alone!" Banyan exclaimed.

"Do as I say," Jin hissed, "or I'll tell the whole village you're a coward who refuses to protect his wife."

With a heavy heart, Banyan went to Ming's land, cut down all the bamboo and threw it into the river.

But Ming worked hard and readied her paddy for planting. Her heart rejoiced when the rice grew tall and strong.

One day a letter arrived.

Dearest wife,

I have wonderful news. By Heaven's grace, I struck it rich with a lucky find of gold and will return on the next ship.

Your loving husband,
Bamboo

Two months passed, then three, then four.

Ming harvested her crops, and the bamboo grove grew back. But her husband did not return.

Ming worried.

Early one morning a runner dashed into the village and called for Ming.

"I bring bad news," he said. "Your husband's ship sank at sea."

Ming was sad, but she refused to weep. In her heart she knew that Bamboo would return just as he had promised.

Every evening Ming went to the dock to wait for Bamboo.

And every evening the villagers brought her food. "Eat," they said. "Keep up your strength."

One evening, Jin followed Ming to the dock. "Your dinner smells wonderful," Jin exclaimed, helping herself to the food the villagers had brought. She ate so greedily that she didn't see her son fall into the river. Ming saw the splash, dove in and saved him. But a strong current swept her away.

Ming floated downstream until a pair of hands reached into the river and pulled her ashore.

"Ming, I've come back," sang out a familiar voice.

There was Bamboo, alive and well. Ming hugged him tightly.

"They told me your ship sank at sea."

"Yes, many lives were lost. I almost drowned, weighed down by a sack of gold on my back. But after I cut it loose, I rose to the surface and found myself surrounded by thick bamboo poles. I grabbed one and floated along with my shipmates. Soon a passing ship rescued us. Look, I brought the poles back."

"They came from our farm. Your brother cut them down and sent them to you."

The next morning Ming and Bamboo returned to their village. When Jin saw them, she fell to her knees and begged for mercy.

"Sister-in-law, I was wrong. I made your life painful, yet you saved my little boy. I was nasty, but you were kind. Please forgive me," she cried.

"Of course I do," said Ming, warmly embracing her.

When people from the nearby villages heard about Ming's bamboo and how many lives it had saved, they came to see the magical crop.

"This will make the best ladders!" exclaimed the carpenters.

"This will make the best scaffolding," said the builders.

"This will make the best carrying-poles!" cried the porters.

"We'll pay you well!" they all shouted.

Bamboo and Ming shared their good fortune with Banyan and Jin. And as their bamboo grove flourished, so did their family.